Life

The Good things of Life

Life

The Good things of Life

ISBN/EAN: 9783741191756

Manufactured in Europe, USA, Canada, Australia, Japa

Cover: Foto ©Andreas Hilbeck / pixelio.de

Manufactured and distributed by brebook publishing software
(www.brebook.com)

Life

The Good things of Life

THE GOOD THINGS

OF

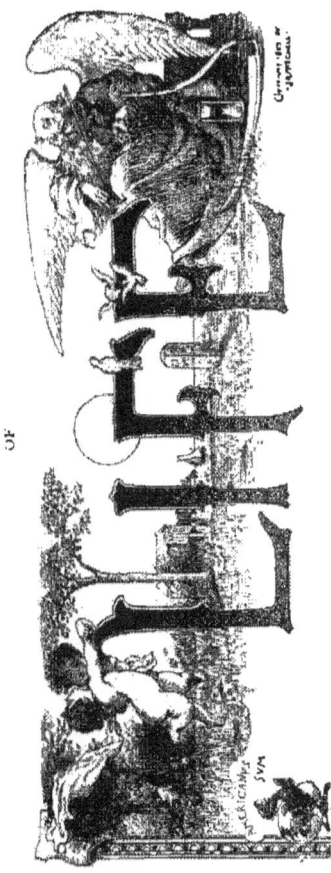

LIFE

SEVENTH SERIES

"'Tis trifles such as these
That make a happy life."

NEW YORK
FREDERICK A. STOKES COMPANY
MDCCCXL

REASON ENOUGH.

She: How conceitedly that man talks. Is he an actor?

He: Worse than that! He's an amateur actor.

PRESENCE OF MIND.

Prodigy Pen-&-Inker: IT IS EVIDENT THAT WOMAN OVER THERE PAINTS.

Bishop Gullem: SHE IS MY SISTER.

Prodigy Pen-&-Inker: I WAS GOING TO SAY IT IS EVIDENT SHE PAINTS FROM THE INTEREST SHE TAKES IN THAT YOUNG ARTIST.

REHEARSING FOR CHARADES.

Freddy: NOW, CHARLIE, YOU MUST PROPOSE TO ANGELINE (*in her sixth scene*), AND ANGIE, YOU MUST REFUSE HIM. IT SHALL BE "PARADISE LOST." SEE?

Charlie (thoughtfully): THEY'LL NEVER GUESS IT IN THE WORLD.

COMPENSATIONS.

Accepted Suitor: WON'T YOU FIND IT AWKWARD WHEN YOU MEET YOUR OTHER TWO HUSBANDS IN HEAVEN?

Interesting Widow: I DO NOT EXPECT TO MEET EITHER OF THEM THERE.

THE NEW HORSE.

Miss Pelham. WHY, MICHAEL, JUST LOOK AT THE SADDLE!

Michael (new to the business). YES'LL, FOIND YEE'LL GIT OF FASTER THAT WAY, MISS. HE'S A SLOW, OBSTHRAIN BASTE FRONTWAYS, BUT HE'S A DIVIL FOR BACKIN'!

Mr. Top Henry : WILL YOU SHARE MY LOT, PENELOPE?

Penelope : YES, IF THERE IS A BROWN STONE FRONT ON IT.

A KINDNESS.

She could never content to marry this young clergyman, and she divines the object of his visit from his trepidation. She has a bright idea, and rings for Dawson.

"DAWSON, TELL MR. STEVENSON AND GENERAL SWIFT THAT I WILL JOIN THEM FOR A LITTLE POKER AT THE USUAL HOUR THIS EVENING. AND, DAWSON, BE SURE AND PUT MORE RUM IN THE PUNCH THAN YOU DID YESTERDAY."

"HAS CHARLEY A SISTER?"

"NO, BUT HE IS GOING TO HAVE ONE AS SOON AS HE PROPOSES TO ME."

10

A JUSTIFICATION.

Aunt Deborah (religiously): WOE TO THE MEN WHO MARRY THOSE FLYBELLE GIRLS; FOR THEY TOIL NOT, NEITHER DO THEY SPIN.

Miss Daisy: OH, AUNT DEBORAH! YOU WRONG THEM, INDEED YOU DO! I MEET THEM OFTEN AT DANCES.

"SINCE YOU HAVE INSISTED ON TRYING ON MY HAT, MRS MABEL, I SHALL CERTAINLY CLAIM THE FORFEIT."

"I DON'T KNOW WHAT YOU MEAN, SIR; AND BESIDES, THIS ISN'T A GOOD PLACE; THEY CAN SEE US FROM THE HOTEL."

Penelope Peachblow : How do you do, Mrs. Plantagenet?

Mrs. Plantagenet : You must excuse me, but I do not think we have ever met.

Penelope Peachblow : Yes; last week, at Mrs. Westerley's.

Mrs. Plantagenet (with increasing coolness): You have the advantage of me.

Penelope Peachblow : I think I have, Mrs. Plantagenet—in eyesight, memory, and manner. Good afternoon.

ON THEIR WEDDING JOURNEY.

She: This is Minerva.
He: Was she married?
She: No, she was the Goddess of Wisdom.

Mr. Jonathan Trump: You are charming to-night.

Miss Penelope Peckskrew: Indeed! What nice things you men say! Mr. Brown just told me the same thing.

Mr. Jonathan Trump (anxious to depreciate his rival): Of course, you don't believe he meant it!

HOW SHE KNEW.

He: WHAT MADE YOU THINK THAT PICTURE IN THE EXHIBITION WAS MINE? YOU MUST BE A JUDGE OF STYLE, BECAUSE IT WAS UNSIGNED.

She (modestly): YOU FLATTER ME. I REALLY DIDN'T KNOW IT WAS YOURS UNTIL I SAW EVERYBODY LAUGHING AT IT.

MOST UNFORTUNATE.

Simpson (tremulously): EMMA, DARLING, SAY YES, AND THERE WILL BE ANOTHER ——
Newsboy (outside): BIG BREACH OF PROMISE CASE! EXTRA!

Mr. Jonathan Tramp. WHAT'S THE MATTER WITH YOUNG DARLINGTON? HE'S GOING INTO THE CONSERVATORY WITH DOLLY FLICKER, AS PALE AS A GHOST.

Miss Penelope Pemfather. GOING INTO A DECLINE, I TAKE IT, FROM WHAT I KNOW OF DOLLY.

TWO HEROIC SOULS.

"DEAR GEORGE, I DEEM IT ONLY JUST TO TELL YOU THAT I AM NOT THE RICH GIRL THE WORLD THINKS ME. MY FATHER'S INCOME IS SMALLER THAN IT WAS BEEN, AND MY OWN PRIVATE FORTUNE, FROM MY LOSSES ON THE TURF, YIELDS LESS THAN THIRTY THOUSAND A YEAR."

"LOLO, DEAR, DO YOU THINK ME A FORTUNE-HUNTER—THAT FILTHY LUCRE INFLUENCES MY LOVE FOR YOU? NEVER! I LOVE YOU ALL THE MORE FOR YOUR POVERTY."

HE HAD BEEN A WEEK IN PARIS.

"Do you speak English?"

"No, Señor!"

"Parlez vous Français?"

"Oui, oui, Monsieur."

"Well, hang it, I wish I could!"

THE WISE VIRGIN.

Perdita (knowingly). I CANNOT. I WILL NOT MARRY YOU, ALFRED, AGAINST YOUR MOTHER'S WISH.

Alfred: I WISH YOU WERE NOT SO SENSITIVE.

Perdita: IT IS NOT BECAUSE I AM SENSITIVE; IT IS BECAUSE YOUR FATHER'S ESTATE IS LEFT AT HER DISPOSAL.

BEHIND THE TIMES.

"WE WOULD LIKE TO SEE YOUR MOTHER, IF SHE IS NOT ENGAGED."

Servant-girl: ENGAGED! GOODNESS, SHE WAS ENGAGED LONG AGO, AND GOT MARRIED BEFORE I WAS BORN.

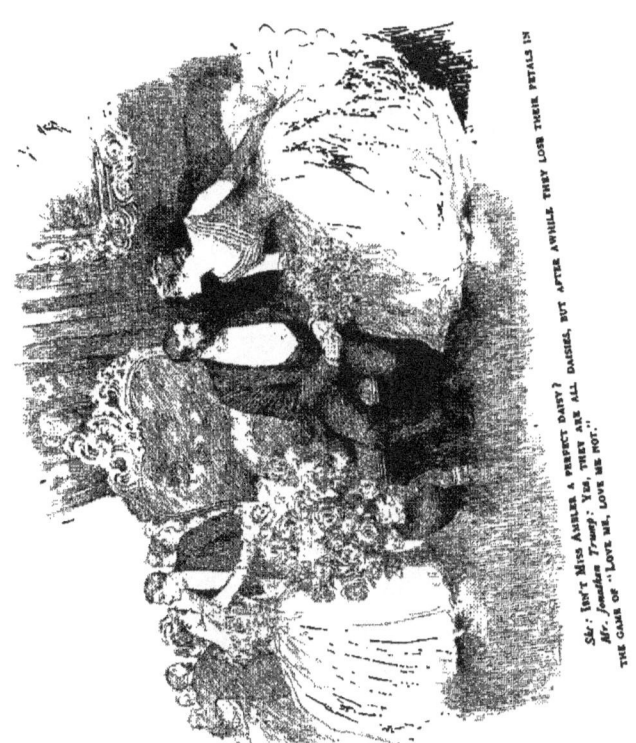

She: Isn't Miss Ashler a perfect daisy?

Mr. Jonadan Tramp: Yes, they are all daisies, but after awhile they lose their petals in the game of "Love me, love me not."

A BARE POSSIBILITY.

Miss A.: I THINK I SHALL GO AS CLEOPATRA, BUT DON'T KNOW WHERE TO GO FOR THE COSTUME.
Mrs. A.: YOU WILL FIND ALL YOU NEED AT TIFFANY'S.

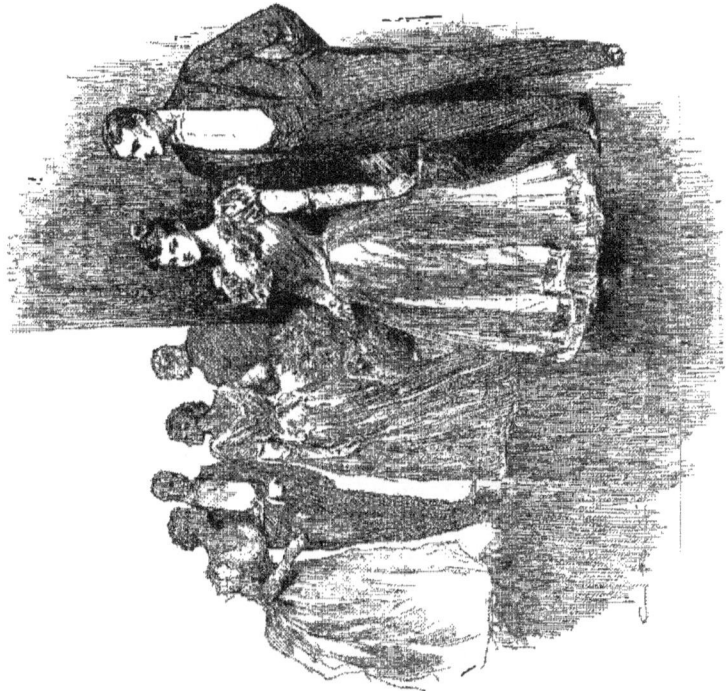

THE FORESIGHTED MAIDEN.

Urgent Suitor. WITH ANY SORT OF MANAGEMENT, WE COULD CERTAINLY KEEP ALIVE ON $800 A YEAR.

She. YES, DEAR; BUT I WOULD SOONER BE COMFORTABLY DEAD.

29

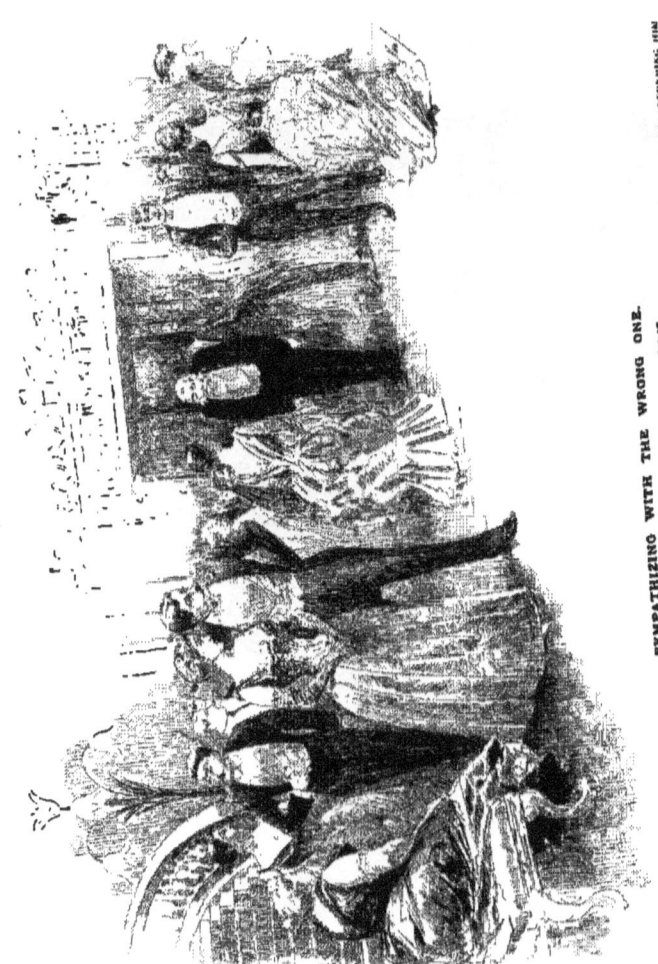

SYMPATHIZING WITH THE WRONG ONE.

SHE: WHAT A SHAME MR. IVISON SHOULD BE SO INTEMPERATE! HE IS JUST RUINING HIMSELF BY IT.

HE: RUINING HIMSELF! IT'S THE RICHEST THING IN EVER DID. HE IS JUST ENGAGED TO A HALF-A-MILLION GAL WHO IS BY SY IN ASTONISHING HIM

30

AFTER THE PLAY.

Mr. Penthington (confident amateur): WELL, MISS PEACHBLOW, HOW DID YOU LIKE IT?

Miss Penelope Peachblow: YOU MADE-UP AND PLAYED YOUR PART BEAUTIFULLY. BUT YOU MUST BE TIRED OF HEARING THAT. I KNOW WHEN I ACTED LIKE A DRIVELLING IDIOT, LAST WINTER, EVERYBODY RUSHED UP TO COMPLIMENT ME UNTIL I WAS BORED TO DEATH.

THE SOLID PAST.

Fair Home Rose: WHAT A PITY, DEAR, YOU ARE ENGAGED SO YOUNG. YOU WILL NEVER HAVE THE FUN OF REFUSING A MAN.

Bud: NO, NO! I'VE HAD THE FUN OF ACCEPTING ONE.

Proud Father : Do you think he looks like me?
Sympathetic Visitor : Yes, poor little thing.

COMING AWAY.

His Lordship: IT WAS JOLLY ENOUGH BUT—ER—BUT WHAT A BEASTLY CROWD. THE SCUM OF EUROPE, I SHOULD SAY.

Mr. F.: THE SCUM OF EUROPE! THEY ARE THE ÉLITE OF NEW YORK!

His Lordship: WHAT'S THE DIFFERENCE, IF YOU ONLY GO BACK A LITTLE?

A NATURAL ANXIETY.

Mrs. Tuthill. I SAW YOUR WIFE OUT RIDING WITH ANOTHER MAN THIS AFTERNOON.

Mr. Tubbs (anxiously). YOU DID! DID THEY HAVE MY HORSE?

KNOWLEDGE IS POWER, BUT IT'S NOT MONEY.

Miss Penelope Pennbligge: WHO IS THAT?

Mr. Jonathan Tramp: OH, THAT'S PROFESSOR DIGBY, WHO KNOWS EVERYTHING. HE'S CONSIDERED ONE OF THE MOST PROFOUND SCHOLARS IN AMERICA.

Miss Penelope Pennbligge: WELL, WHY DOESN'T HE HAVE HIS HAIR CUT?

Mr. Jonathan Tramp: HE CAN'T AFFORD IT.

TABLE D'HÔTE ON THE LAKE OF COMO.

"DON'T YOU, THEN, EVER WASH HERE?"

"OUI, DYAM, NO! I ONLY SCRATCH AND RUB!"

Miss Tomkins, overhearing, leaves the table abruptly much disgusted. She afterwards hears they are members of the Royal British Water Color Society who were discussing the technique of their profession.

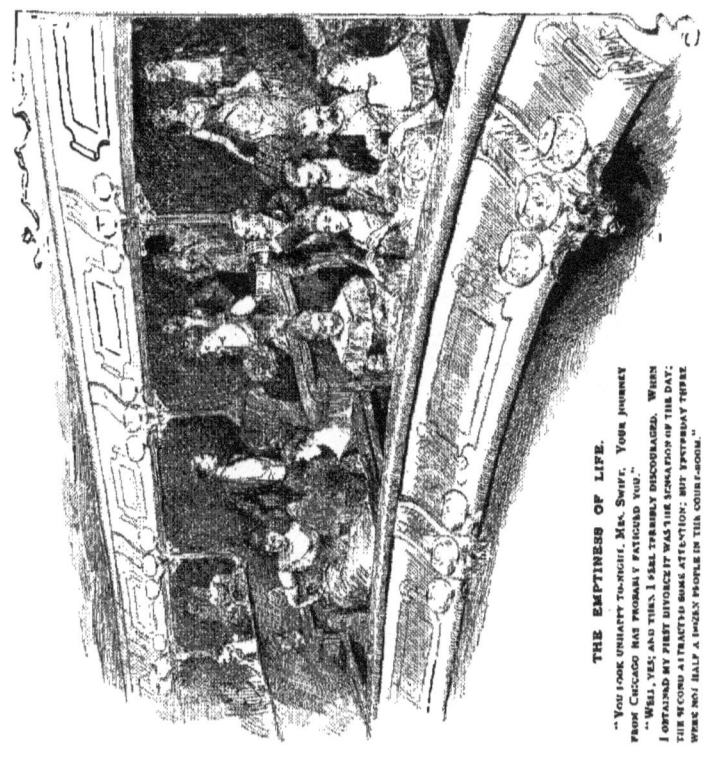

THE EMPTINESS OF LIFE.

"You look unhappy to-night, Mrs. Swift. Your journey from Chicago has probably fatigued you."

"Well, yes; and then, I feel terribly discouraged. When I obtained my first divorce it was the sensation of the day; the second attracted some attention; but yesterday there were not half a dozen people in the court-room."

Pretty (but unsuccessful) Rival. AND DO YOU REALLY THINK HE LOVES YOU?

The Fiancée: OH, YES, AS LOVE GOES IN THESE DEGENERATE DAYS. I EVEN THOUGHT HE WAS GOING TO KISS ME LAST NIGHT.

The Rival: HE TOLD JACK HE WANTED TO, BUT COULDN'T.

MORE IMPORTANT.

"How could you think of falling in love with such a homely fellow? His figure is something awful."

"Yes, but he has a lovely one at the bank."

IN FOR IT.

Mr. Bloomingdale Ward (desperately, after being "stuck" for the last half-dance). ER—WILL YOU EXCUSE ME, MISS AUTUMN?
Miss Autumn (slightly deaf). WITH PLEASURE! WHAT IS IT, A WALTZ?

A RESULT OF CULTURE.

Hostess to Guest: Mrs. Bacon, I want to introduce you to Mrs. Day, a new arrival in Boston, and a charming woman. She is just coming up from supper. She is my next-door neighbor.

Mrs. B.: Oh, don't, I beg of you! Sh—

41

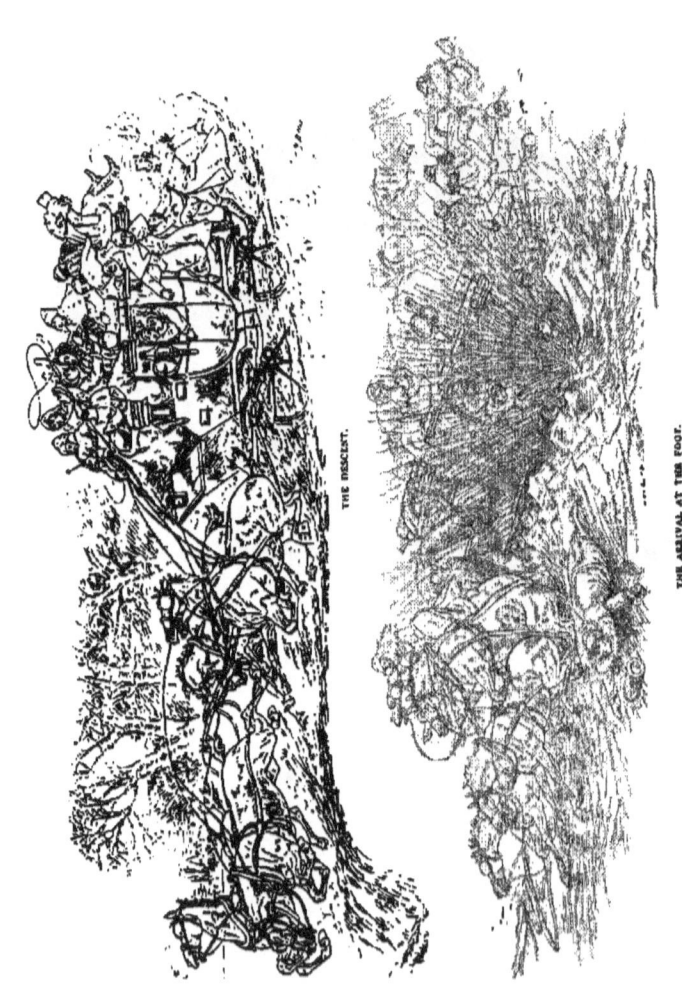

THE DESCENT.

THE ARRIVAL AT THE FOOT.

DISCOURAGING.

Uncle James: WELL, BOBBY, ARE YOU GAINING ANY PRIZES AT SCHOOL NOWADAYS?

Bobby: NO, SIR; THE OTHER FELLOWS GET THEM ALL.

Uncle James: BUT YOU'LL KEEP ON TRYING, OF COURSE.

Bobby: WHAT'S THE USE? THE OTHER FELLOWS KEEP ON TRYING, TOO!

TO SUIT EVERY TASTE.

Miss A.: Don't you find New York society rather empty and unsatisfactory?

Mr. S.: Not necessarily. You can take your choice in that respect. There is the Bohemian set, all brains and no style; Society proper, with a fair amount of each; and the Four Hundred, all style and no brains.

He : Where did you get that suit of armor?

She : That belonged to my great-great grandfather.

He (who knows the family history): Oh, yes; to keep the flies off while he was ploughing?

47

A DISTINCT DECLINE.

Mr. B.: THE BROWNING CULT HAS RATHER SUBSIDED IN YOUR CITY, HAS IT NOT?

Mrs. L. (from Chicago). YES, INDEED! NOW THAT WE HAVE GOT ON TO HIS CURVES, IT IS SCARCELY AN EXAGGERATION TO SAY THAT BROWNING IS ALREADY IN THE SOUP.

THE PENALTY OF PRIDE.

He: And so you're really going to marry that professor! You, the beauty of a thousand encounters, how did you ever come to accept him?

Her Cousin (from Boston): Why, you see, he proposed in Greek, and when I refused him I got mixed on my negatives and—Mercieful!—accepted him, and now I'm too proud to acknowledge my blunder. Oh, I'm his for life!

IN AMERICA.

"I HEAR YOU ARE GOING TO BE MARRIED."
"NO; I'M ONLY ENGAGED."

AT WEST POINT.

Cadet Mars (soon to graduate): MISS LIGHTFOOT—ARABELLA—COULD YOU EVER CONSENT TO LEAVE THE LUXURIES OF YOUR NEW YORK HOME TO GO FAR, FAR AWAY TO THE WEST AND SHARE A SOLDIER'S STERNER LOT—TO BE HIS GUARDIAN ANGEL—TO MAKE HIS HOME A HEAVEN?

Miss Lightfoot (with drooping lashes and crimsoning cheeks): YES, GEORGE, I THINK I COULD.

Cadet Mars: WELL—ER—WELL, MY ROOM-MATE, SAM JOHNSON, IS GOING INTO THE CAVALRY. I'LL SPEAK TO HIM ABOUT IT.

Bishop Gadbee: MISS AUTUMN, I HEAR YOU ARE AN EARNEST STUDENT OF THE BIBLE. WHAT, IN YOUR OPINION, IS THE MOST INTERESTING LINE OF HOLY WRIT?

Miss Autumn (promptly): "BEHOLD, THE BRIDEGROOM COMETH!"

Mr. Bloomingdale Ward (tremulously, after venturing a kiss): I—I BEG PARDON. I DIDN'T MEAN TO. I——

Miss Dolly Flicker (tearfully): IF YOU HAD BEEN SINCERE, I MIGHT HAVE FORGIVEN YOU.

Miss Photogent De Vere: THAT MAN'S ATTENTIONS TO ME ARE MOST OFFENSIVE, AND MR. HAS THE REPUTATION OF BEING A FORTUNE HUNTER. DO YOU SUPPOSE IT IS PAPA'S WEALTH THAT ALLURES HIM?

Miss Dolly Fisher (thoughtfully): WHY, WHAT ELSE CAN IT BE?

HOW HE LOST HER.

Miss Antwerp. BUT WOULD YOU CONTINUE TO LOVE ME WHEN I BECAME OLD AND UGLY?

Mr. Pendleton (enthusiastically). I LOVE YOU NOW, DEAREST!

THE SAGACIOUS MAIDEN.

He: I DON'T SEE WHY YOU WON'T MARRY A MAN WITHOUT CAPITAL, IF HE HAS A GOOD SALARY.

MOTHER EVE MARRIED A GARDENER.

She: YES, AND THE FIRST THING HE DID WAS TO LOSE HIS SITUATION!

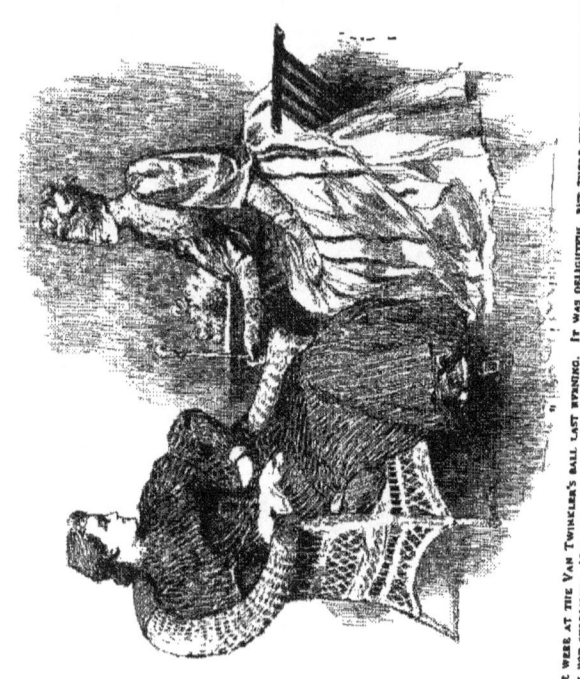

"We were at the Van Twinkler's ball last evening. It was delightful, but there were very few men."
"I'm not surprised. My husband says that men are very scarce among the Four Hundred."

THE USES OF WORDS.

Lawyer's Clerk: WILL YOU TAKE A CHAIR, MISS?

Boston Girl: NO, THANK YOU; I WOULDN'T KNOW WHAT TO DO WITH IT. BUT I'LL SIT DOWN, IF I MAY.